D0618396

"Well, there's your problem."

"Well, there's your problem."

CARTOONS BY EDWARD KOREN

Pantheon Books, New York

For Nat and Sasha

By the same author
Do You Want To Talk About It?
Are You Happy?

Compilation Copyright © 1980 by Edward Koren

All rights reserved under International and Pan-American Copyright Conventions.
Published in the United States by Pantheon Books, a division of Random House, Inc., New York, and simultaneously in Canada by Random House of Canada Limited, Toronto.

All of the drawings in this collection appeared originally in The New Yorker *and were Copyrighted © 1976, 1977, 1978, 1979, and 1980 by The New Yorker Magazine, Inc.*

LIBRARY OF CONGRESS CATALOGING IN PUBLICATION DATA
Koren, Edward. "Well, there's your problem."
Cartoons. 1. American wit and humor, Pictorial. I. Title.
NC1429.K62A4 1980 741.5'973 79-1972
ISBN 0-394-51266-9

Manufactured in the United States of America
FIRST EDITION

"He loves to be petted."

"Ah! It's the Woodwind family!"

"I love to be alive. It's fun."

me

"I'm sorry, I can't cope with that now!"

"When they talked about the cultural scene out here, they never told me about you."

HISTORIC HOUSE
FROM 1953 TO 1961, LARRY PANE LIVED AND WORKED HERE WRITING SOME OF TELEVISION'S MOST CELEBRATED COMMERCIALS, INCLUDING THE NATSO SPAGHETTI SPOT AND THE FAMOUS SASHA BIRD FOOD CAMPAIGN

"When the children have all grown up, we hope to move back to the city."

"Sweetie, will you help me with my tie?"

"Just to set the record straight, I'm leaving you because you never turn your body to the net, because you don't have a smooth swing, and because your forehand, backhand, and volley are inadequate!"

"Oh, excuse me! I thought you were somebody I know."

"Our philosophy here at Dandelion Motors is to treat the total car."

"We got a complaint that his steak au poivre was dry and overcooked, his chicken vinaigrette was prepared poorly in a sticky sweet-and-sour onion sauce that bordered on the inedible, and his leaf-spinach-with-mushroom salad was crudely seasoned."

"It shrank."

"And what do you do to maintain your cardiovascular fitness, Miss Holt?"

FOOD & DRINK
SORRY
NO BARE
FEET

"You're terribly cute for someone who's fortyish."

"I have the honor to present the man who has done so much to popularize this instrument."

"Morris knows how to fix his own car."

"The reason you all are becoming extinct is that you can't take a joke."

"Let us defer to the judgment of our oenologist."

THE
PERFECT
COUPLE

"Alexandra, you possess a very large talent."

"The people who admire and appreciate you are on this side, and the ones who don't care so much for you are on the other."

"What are you in the mood for?"

METAPHOR FOR ASPIRATION
METAPHOR FOR LYRICISM
METAPHOR FOR DEATH AND DECAY
METAPHOR FOR GROWTH AND CHANGE
METAPHOR FOR LIMITS
METAPHOR FOR THE POSSIBLE
METAPHOR FOR STABILITY
METAPHOR FOR THE EPHEMERAL
METAPHOR FOR LOVE

"I'm a fresh-vegetable fan."

"I can never get it straight. Was William Carlos Williams the doctor or the insurance man?"

"Are you someone in authority?"

"Take it all off."

"It's me—Mr. Rhythm himself!"

"We still can't decide whether she's more a Hillary or an Allison."

"Good morning, Mr. Dolman. In for your twelve-thousand-mile checkup?"

HAPPY ANNIVERSARY
3 WONDERFUL YEARS
6 SO-SO YEARS
2 ROTTEN YEARS

"Rick Hoffman, six miles a day, I'd like you to meet Brent Evans, ten miles a day."

"Excuse me. What is the name of that dish?"

COMMONPLACE.
TRUISM
CLICHÉ
PLATITUDE.
BANALITY.
BROMIDE.

"I fell in love with you the first time I heard your message on the answering machine."

"This is an outrage to the cooking public!"

"How long have you and Charlie been together?"

"Good morning. Kirk, Kirk, Kirk & Kirk."

"Here we are, Stephen—ready to party."

"Do you, Jane, and you, Jonathan, jointly vow to split the royalties, paperback rights, book-club proceeds, and movie options with each other in the event that the marriage dissolves and results in a work of fiction or nonfiction based on this union?"

"If you don't like the tempest, get out of the teapot."

"I think it's wonderful to be so direct with your anger."

SECONAL
AMYTAL
PHENO-
BARBITAL
NEMBUTAL
TUINAL

"This is an imaginative new concept in the use of leisure time."

"See anyone you know?"

"It may be presumptuous of me, but I would like to undertake a summary of Peter's ideas."

"Jerry, I'm beginning to think it's wrong that all our fun is based on the combustion of hydrocarbons."

"I used to think you were a Renaissance man, Michael, but now I think you're a Neanderthal."

"Ezra, I'm not inviting you to my birthday party, because our relationship is no longer satisfying to my needs."

"Let's disco, you old stodge!"

"You are my grass roots."

"And this? Trash or treasure?"

"Well, for your information, I happen to love nature."

"Daniel has become indifferent to weather conditions."

"You're right, Melissa, it does need salt. And also oregano, basil, thyme, and possibly a pinch of chervil."

"This is my only New York appearance this year."

"I love the honesty of your lyric."

"Pop, you've got to be more supportive of Mom and more willing to share with her the day-to-day household tasks. Mom, you have to recognize Pop's needs and be less dependent on him for your identity."

"This is my new old man."

"Isn't it wonderful that I'm so angry at women and you're so angry at men!"

"John and I have decided that we're sick of hearing about women and their problems."

"Nat is here with us through the gracious courtesy of Ahsas Records."

"I think what people are going to say is 'Wow!'"

"I'm never bored! I've got my pottery, my plants, my weaving, and my man."

"According to the Times, I'm 'superb.'"

"Michael welcomes contrasting points of view."

I'M
SINGLE

"Come on in, Donald, and reacquaint yourself with the meaning of fun."

"The woman who ordered the poulet chasseur would like to come in and rap about it."

"No, Philip, it's not just me. We're all incredibly angry!"

"I'd like you to meet our friend the protein."

"This is Alex, of Chicken Alex."

"I'm sorry, I can't talk. I've got company."

"Hi! I'm all natural."

"Your depression is contagious."

"Oh, there's Freddie. He knows the best places to suffer."

while you wait
OUR EXPERTS
REALLY ARE
EXPERTS

"Wait, I know what's different. Your hair's curlier."

BOB BINKER
BOB AND JUDITH 1947-1953
BOB AND PAT JUNE 1953 ~ SEPT. 1953
BOB AND SUSAN 1955 ~ 1965
BOB AND FRAN 1970 ~ 1972
KATE LANDE
KATE AND HAL 1950 ~ 1952
KATE AND DICK 1952 ~ 1957
KATE AND BILL 1960 ~ 1967
KATE AND HENRY 1967 ~ 1972
BOB AND KATE 1973-

"Will you share my dream with me, Alexandra? A few acres somewhere, a couple of sheep, a couple of goats, some chickens..."

"So this is your young man, Melissa!"

"Well, there's your problem!"

"I'd like to thank all my friends for their tremendous love and criticism."

"So this is the famous Sarah of the mustard-mayonnaise clam dip!"

"Would you be a dear and fetch me a toad?"

"I love your husband, Louise. He's very male without being macho."

"It's the most assertive thing I've ever done."

"You have a wonderful body."

"Are you dating anyone seriously?"

"We live a few miles from here in an architecturally significant former gas station."

ANOTHER
BEAUTIFUL
HISTORIC HOUSE
WAITING
TO BE
RESTORED
PROVIDENCE PRESERVATION SOCIETY

"I know all about you and your pâté from the New York Times!"

"Now, this is a very new variety, which some people are having trouble relating to."

"New York is a constant nourishment for Daniel."

FROM THE DESK OF J. A. FARROW

"The night woods
Listen attentively
To the owl's
discourse,
While at dawn
The grosbeak
Elaborates the lightening sky
With musical significance."

"It's a look I believe in."

STOP PAY TOLL
SUGGESTED
CONTRIBUTION
.50

"Spain—overrated. France—overrated. Switzerland! Germany! Belgium! England! Italy! All overrated!"

"We're semi-frantic today."

TIME
HAS NOT
BEEN
KIND
TO YOU

"Well, I see that our time is just about up."